R

**ceremonies
in
bachelor
space**

E

ISBN 978-0-578-67108-6

This edition published in 2020 by:

Tough Poets Press
Arlington, Massachusetts 02476
U.S.A.

www.toughpoets.com

ceremonies in bachelor space

russell edson

tough poets press
arlington
massachusetts

SONGS

for the
Twilight hours
and flowers
and You

How east man vesper west goes how each man to reach men belies
the prime limb who resists stays in half phase of lambs liable to
limbo.

Rosa late-light in east night by limb's bray by wind's thin laugh out
of the welkin out of grey in fail-light by now the braille light by the
ailing rote of tree's re-leaf of leaves rote fall on curfew earth.

When limbs fire all day begun la vine loops in emerald light the Tit-
ian trails melt rosa day is ends oscuro where the frau fruit soars on
the fringes of the shores of Columbus sailing arc arse o'er domina
into furrow at thigh's narrow.

Do you remember great sea fall when both broke asunder leaf shattered by the neck of approach and world is made all blossom's leaf and stem or vine were massed and all flows begun by heat site sun site and the flow begun be leaf flight in noon light.

Where man rose among the draughts of leaf life and felled among the bonds fell among the swarms and things enthralled by the thrashes and thrusts of the thrushes among the thrum branchy threads where sun shines in the short grass in the grief-fall where man or all may force in the grand allure past the leaning door.

The dross drowse leaving where lifedrome ends the weavings all gone to thrum reveals now flight that hence thwarted the blending is blent to one projet to swaddling flax from all flood that facts the fruit and rives the coupling the down tall trees and sons
when will white become the sun the branches brawl their leaves by bounty fruit when will **divide** and scarce growth renew.

When will we descend by goldenrod past vermillion east to rise when two hands go when lovers random in the snow will re-occur when willows will reflect by vast light lost by land light cast
where willed by wish thrown by famine trails that leads asunder to projet-wonder
by vandal or the fickle (. . . as they will contend) the candle or the sickle yet time they come to earthen braille where o'er the maids will spill as ere
wan child gone grey by Sol's gross green.

p. s. The mal-force of the yeast blom the ground o'er cast with the mal grown the carolers in hedge growth commence sing that Sol that falls carrier of the pollen whore acrid when winter will be come how man closes in calendar.

Notions
of
the
Saint

In meerschaum white, in the clouded day—For the day seen white, makes it time for the saint, apropo tor the saint

When the children on the banks of the river, slowed by mood, is it time that a saint—is it time for a saint?

A female saint who walks familiar streets in autumn, past vacant houses to the river.

Oh, sky, tremendous by width; made more of this by land so flat.

For the saint is come now, and the mist offers over land, floating by attic windows.

The saint is come—And children with sandwich and milk— And they try to keep the sadness away, but all becomes mute and dumb-show. So, likely, that the bland smile of a saint welcomes its own welcome.

In a flax white gown, faded roses on her temple, and lips that fade in the mist-shift, with little, slight-colored flowers she proceeds. An accidental stain of previous wine or other, makes her seem little out of the domicile.

Thoughts of home invade the wilderness, and smiles of the homefolk. For the saint, very like a beetle in shape, with her veils and the mist that shapes us easily, stands with her bland smile.

And the children swear that they will lay down their lives: such is the magic that saints bring in the mist.

And, as this is unwant, they dedicate their activities, modified by the word.

And the saint ascends to amuse the children. And as her feet disappear into the sky the boys jump upon each other with embarrassment and wrestle. The girls imitate the saint.

For they have been visited with a most rare and divine sight, which becomes too much to believe. Which, were they to believe, would forward them in the saint's wake. **And they vanish, and their mothers call in vain**, and find them late for the thickness of the fog off the river.

And in the late evening, when the children sit to supper—

The white cloth, with meat and vegetables and bread and milk and gravy and navy beans, and set to the middle with twilight flowers, becomes a saint laid on her back, beset with food. Passive to the threat, so in the fork and other implement in service.

It is her white skin where the boys and his father eat from plates set upon each of her mammary glands.

The salt and pepper lie in her bellybutton.

The vegetables are laid out on her legs.

The napkins are over her eyes.

The twilight flowers are sticking from her delta.

The gravy is in a pool between her mammary glands.

And the mother has gone to bed with a headache.

The boy and his father eat, conversing softly. They reach deftly for the meat laid between her legs.

In mistake they start to eat the white flesh. Their plates slide off the mammary glands, and still they eat. And the saint dissolves in the digestive tracts of the boy and his father.

They wipe their mouths, and the boy's mother, and his father's wife, descend refreshed.

In the evening the saint wandered in the blue grass wetting the edge of her gown. She flits by the windows with closed eyes, and then walks into the sky.

And in the morning a child is beset by an ever recurring shadow, that turns to left, if the child go left, or right, and again as the child goes. Till, up and down a wall the man of the shadow appears, and the child promises, in its non-action, what the man of the shadow wills.

The child's body tumbles over and over again. Keeping no level or balance, as the man turneth the child, raping its mystery; till, the magic pours red in the mist. Till, where is child, all tumbled and nondescript?

And the angels prod each other as the nondescript child walks into the sky.

Anxiously, the mother doth all things the child know.

And, as the **man** approach, she hails the plumber, or the tuna-fish man, whatever. And **he** asks of the boy, still with the taste of the last moments **he** has spent tearing the carefully kept child, of this woman.

The child looks over the rail of heaven and cries, "He has killed me; for what, I don't know—He, mother, he . . ."

The blood on the **man's** hands **he** says is **his** own, and the boy's mother washes the **man's** hands and bandages them and sits to wait for her **angel**, for he is due from school.

And an old hag makes bitter the wax of a young girl's innocent flame.

But, the hag catches-fire from the innocence, and delivers the child from the bitter wax.

And, the mist clears away, leaving the neighborhood to the sun.

And, childish fancy weaves, most lovely tales to the old, who are refreshed and more willed to live.

And, the families eat their lunches, and the talk at these meetings is gay and promising.

The sun drops into an amber twilight, and the warm sky breathes gently over the neighborhood, and all assume their beds. Some to embrace and other to lie alone with the hope of night-time-embraces, which shall for them, embrace all the night. And these now, embrace themselves.

And the saint wanders in the happy dreams of the young wearing her bland and professional smile.

And finally, utter black and no coit.

the
fear

I am going to the hills. I have finished my stay here. They ask me where I will go; I do not know; but, that I crave hills, I shall be that place of hills.

How I miss this landscape—the shadow-drift of the area. Shadows gaining into the mind, engraved there as scenery of the mind.

Children going past the windows look in, and my things being gathered and made into collections for a journey. Dust, dust, letters and children's eyes. Tears administered to a certain emotion. Here is a certain place, and the hills to go; and why am I going?: That I do not stay.

If I could understand fate as a witch . . . She is standing by a stove; and many believing, believe her to be mother cooking children's supper. She is squeezing different herbs in different pots: "This for the good boy, and this, for the good girl, and **this**, for the bad boy . . ."

I do not believe; and not this at all.

Papers, dust . . . child I'm not sure, perhaps to the hills, you must trust me, you must trust me to be.

At forty, I understand, we're much older; when I am so, we shall be enfeebled and have tears for all emotions, and be quite aware of the shadow we now permit. Shadow to keep us safe shadow that we are used to.

The cows in the last weeks have been driven to feed in the fields, . . . snow is gone. Back to the barns near the night they are driven, passing windows with their quiet voices.

What shall I take with me? Letters, of course, all of my clothing; I could not think: others wearing my clothes. Clothes that hid me more than kept me warm; now to keep an unhiding farmer? These farmers, without introspection, have found nothing, it seems, to hide. And could one wearing my clothes learn to hide what I have hid? And am I only that which I hide? If so, would that make any and all who wear my clothes hiders as me? God forbid!

Here is a print I shall give a child, and a pencil too, for a child. Here is leaving when I do not want to leave. Leaf, leaf—you have grown so lately; I understand with a chemically knowing mind what you have done my green leaf.

Shall it be a train, a car, bicycle, or merely a knowledge, a knowing, which is above all the thing I wish to be of.

Goodbye, yes, goodbye. Perhaps I should have been a teacher, should be leaving in the fall with immigrant leaves. Not this at all, this is the time when school ends. Sad at leaving, the higher class has graduated. They will be entering universities. Some I am sure will be writers, others will play pianos. They go out, they go out. I am sure we shall read about them in a few years. I am not a teacher.

Under this earth, under this room, under my activity, the miners are digging.

Anybody . . .: Ding-dong, a mouse, ding-ding-dong. I am neither honored or dishonored; nor a mouse, that after three years dies embittered. Have I gained love? How many women with how many fish, who've eaten how many fish, who've eaten how many sea-plants, who've absorbed how much of the water I've sweated all months of my stay?

Hove I gained love? Yes—sundry beetles have supped on my willing flesh, yea did I feed while I fed.

And to the hills—where the crisp rock shatters, where of the moss, the tree . . . and my weary feet. For I climb, you see, mixing so, in the scenery of the hills.

The scene is ruined, the tree has grown before the landscape, the shaggy feather of a foolish wish. Tree, down to a root, see?, into uninspired pebbled ground. Men of the church walking in black . . . shops . . . However, to be away!, to bring these things into order. However, a letter to be written. However, therefore, I will not leave my clothes for them to wear; not even the needy need hide. Spring, and a passion in the park, where they may use a nickel in the name of coffee; and I may be far away writing a letter. And the same bird, may I see it, were they seeing it; some man shot it, from the hills I may see it.

I may be walking knee-deep in the ferns of a valley. With sudden turn of mind I turn twin leggedly, first one leg and then the other. I turn to climb the hills; I turn in climb from clumps of bush to surer footing of leafen ledges.

I am sure, and so I turn, there: A large grey animal. I turn and see another. I turn, I turn, I turn. With sudden wish I reach the tops of hills. Twined in my journey, twin lobes of my brain, twin legs, twinly organed I am able to rise playing a mouth-organ.

Curiously, lunch earlier in the day! In earlier days I should not have eaten lamb brain. Curiously, lunch earlier in the day has been brain of the lamb. All the time now, and before in the day, since I have eaten it, it has been curious to me the operation I can not see.

I now discover grey animals to be grey boulders, and having lost my fear I shall discipline myself to the climb; in fact, I shall be forced to, since still I climb—Where thought I the height reached, it was not. And I am still in error, since the grey masses are the grey animals—Some sort of grazing animal. They kill but can not eat. They kill by their clumsiness, meaning nothing in murder. Clumsiness being a weapon for the innocents to keep the hills free for the grazing activity.

MOTHER & WOMEN

One night a woman slept in the linear folds of her sheet. The blankets had fallen to the floor. She shuddered from the cold but did not wake. The snow had begun to fall in the evening. She had eaten bread and jam, and having finished her coffee, she put out the lamp and went to bed.
She had abandoned her fear of strangers, wishing now for anybody to come.

A male homosexual had been driven into the night with his desire. And being thoroughly exhausted wished more for the arms of the lover he had set forth to find. He had awakened suddenly and felt his body, squeezing the loneliness from his flesh; But that this did not satisfy him, he wrapped his blanket around himself, broke through the space on the stairs, the door way and along the streets barefooted. He had gone to where the streets end and the fields of snow begin, and across these he made his way. He saw the foolishness of his act, but reasoned to himself with half belief, of finding some silly farm boy at early milking alone in a barn. He stood in the shelter of a stunted fir tree and gathered the blanket under his feet. He could not see any barn. The woman had awakened and pulled the covers on to the bed. She had been long away from home. She asked herself why she slept alone in this low wooden building, why was she here? She stroked her breasts and whispered, "Mother." She let her hands play her full length, feeling at once helpless and childlike and then comforted by the matured woman's shape. Wishing she could crawl

to her own breasts. She wished to press her thighs to the thighs, her face to the face of a young girl, as **she** was. She wrapped her arms around the pillow, pushing her breasts into it, hugging it with her thighs, her mouth at the tip of the pillow, wetting it and sucking it. The male homosexual was walking near by, but he did not see the low wooden building. He was thinking, "Why do these silly farmers sleep so well tonight? . . . Where are their houses? Where are barns . . . even, . . . where are fences? Fickle people, easily could they have built a house there, here, there, here, there, anywhere, mostly here . . . What do I mean?" He screamed, "I'll die, I'll die . . . hey anybody, I'm dying." As he was about to shout again he noticed a low wooden shack, and he said, "Ha," and entered. He whispered in a whisper that had no sex, "Is anybody here?"
"Who is there?"
"I'm lost and cold, could you help me?" He whispered, "Are you a man?"
She thought it best to say she was, for she could not tell what he was, "Yes, I'm a man, what are you?"
He thought a man would accept a woman better than another man. He answered, "I'm a woman, may I stay?"
She whispered, "Stay. Here is my hand."

He laughed and he cried. And when he cried she cried, and they went close to each other. She licked the nipple on his chest and he buried his head in her hair and wept. His hand caressed down her back to her buttocks, into her inner thighs. She moved closer, almost to become in his body. Their murmurs became mixed. "Mother, mother, man the mother . . . before, before the morning. Frightened little mother, boy-like mother."
He is heard to say, "Mother of women, sister, midwife, where we can not love. Midwife in my mother's birth."
They cried and took many parts of each other in their mouths. They hugged one another with their arms and thighs. Seeking no limit, but finding whatever thing they seek.

HER LIMBS LIKE FAWNS, LEAD EYES, CIRCUMFUSING IN TICK-TIDES:
I'M OR TIME'S A BOUNDARY WICK—
ONE DECAYS, AND THAT'S A MEND, SOMEHOW A TREND:
OUT OF THE DENSE, LOCKED DREG THE RESIDUE WALKS RESPLENDENT SEED.

SINE DIE, ONE CAPE FOR ALL. BUT DROWNING IN THE EAST: MY MOTHER'S FLOOD.
NOW WESTER WANE HER WANING AND HER WONDER DONE.
ONE SHAPE FOR THE EVER-STRAYED, WITH THE FLOWER-FINAL: AVID GROWER, EVER LOWER, FLAW ETERNAL.

STEM'S A LYRE, WIND'S A PRAYER—

THE HYMEN EYE, THAT HAS NOT SIGN OR THROAT: TIS THE WE'S OF ARM SICK WITHOUT. TILL THRUM-DARLINGS NARRATE IN FIRE, THE NEVER-COMPLETE DESIRE.
OVER A MATE, BETWEEN KNEE AND KNEE, THE MIRROR OF ME-EVIDENT. HOW I, HOW WE, HOW THEE AT INFANT'S-WAIT, THE DIMPLE OF BIRTH, IN THE QUARRELLING GATES: ICE AND SUN, AMONG THE FRUIT-SKINS OF DAWN, OR THE FRAIL CHILD: TWILIGHT . . . HOW IT IS, THAT WE PART, WORMWARD, OR TO THE SECRET FALL WITH HYMEN'S HURT.

HER LIMBS LIKE FAWNS, LEAD EYES AFRAID . . .
                              WINGS, WINGS WILL WANT US,
WHILE WE WANT THE WITNESS OF THE WINGS, THAT WILL WANT THE WITNESS OF THE WINGS . . .

TO YOU

winter

what after-thought are flowers?—after the fields and the vanes west,
when sun decays among the brain and branch (the branch waked by
the Heavener's breath)
duplication of my organs in the fields—
winter is now—soft now the drone—the evening snow bangs in the
quiet wood. cool prayers in the fading, white white and fading.

winter's fine face lies in coma in the fields. stepping the thaw-flesh
upon the peat eyes, rock eyes, with their warm and heavy ice lids.
sleep my heavy woman winter on the bed of summer sweets:
flowers' night and formal warmth.

Where do the worms mortify the knee of him that loved so well?—
and what fly of summer animates such disbanding of that flesh.
what fly might I have killed . . . ?
summer summer, and he's over; summer's over and my summer
tears are turned to snow; each, the drops are flaking now.
impede the worm, oh woman winter; protect him with my grief.

winterscape is where children pillow-fight till the pillows break:
slower than the loins with love is the snow crawling in the air.
at last, at last the much fallen world is white; in various states of
white.
a moment of simplicity upon the rapes of summer.
there is no fever in the white, the dead and living are in night.
white birds are flying in the mind—the white wind clings erranded
with white, white birds, white and warm birds—white and womb-
flushed herds.

the villager

I have an ugly face though my mother and father were considered good looking. They say, I must be a throwback to some rather ugly ancestor, who, being so long ago, is not remembered by any in the village, though I imagine many in the village sit at night trying to recall the ugly ancestor of mine. Of course it is none of their business; but they feel it is, since all of us in this village are related somewhat to each other, and they feel it is in a way a village blemish. Their thought is obviously totalitarian.

The ugliness on my part has kept me from developing a trade, making me for the most, idle. But outward idleness is not a sign of inward idleness. My ugliness has put me in a position apart from fellows, where I can study them. In many ways I find them stupid, and this to me is a form of ugliness. They have accepted Darwin's theory; but that is as far as they have gone with the new conceptions of the modern age.

I have not been permitted to marry, for fear that my ugliness will spread. And the satisfaction of a woman is also denied me. They have taken all incentive away, and yet they condemn my idleness. I can not leave, for in many ways my thinking is backward, conditioned of course by the common stupidity of the village, which, as I grew up, was imbedded in my mind. And, too, they have a strange pride, that even though I am ugly, unfit to marry, still they wish to keep the family together. In a sense I am still a brother, still a son. Yet with all the knowledge I have, which is a great deal more than anyone in the village, and a great deal less than anyone in the outside world, I can't improve my condition here.

Occasionally I say something considered witty and people laugh. They even break down and say, "That's the funniest remark I've heard in a dog's age." (I think dogs live for fifteen years.) They soon forget, till I make another witty remark. I can't seem to establish a reputation of being wise and witty.

Of late I have taken to sleeping in the fields, which people consider animal-like and unworthy of one of their sons.

They deny me the essentials of happy life, yet feel it their personal sins if I do something out of the ordinary.

A few days ago some gypsies came into our village, one older man and three young women. The young men of the village have been told not to have anything to do with the gypsy women. The elders fear to have any of the village's germs of heredity leave the village with the gypsies. The hell with them! I have slept with one of the gypsy women. And I will say, she has given me, so far, every type of sexual outlet that young men know about. I'm not sure that I love her, but I wish to marry her. The old gypsy man says, "No." For if we marry without the consent of the village the gypsies will forever more be barred from the village. (And our village is very rich etc.)

Hog-wash! I owe no allegiance to my village or the old gypsy. And yet I am afraid to take the step. So now I'm trying to become dreadfully ill, by taking rat poison, but not enough to kill me. If they see me suffering so, they will have to grant me something, won't they? For I am one of their sons. And I have so many wishes. And if I grow a beard I won't be at all bad looking, not at all. But beards are not customary in this village. And I am not an ugly duckling, I am mature, and ugly in my maturity.

But if I have taken rat poison so many times before, I'm sure they are wise by now. Oh, once again and the next time I shall end it all.

prose about Love and notes about That

—And certainly, for the various accounts of her life, was I ready to administer my compass of matter to her.
In the shortness of my chronology, it is fitting I fear not the demolition of her scorn nor her various impoverishing acts upon my person.

I know that this woman shall demand no less of me than life. I, myself, through need which is living, shall demand no less myself, Together, she and I shall take my life.

But what has my life been, but a series of passive smiles to the onrush of the brutal sperm-folk, who could not bring to fruition their violent self-seeds in me. I do not hate them for this, as they do me, but, rather feel sorry I have so disappointed them.
I have wept for them.

———————————

I have committed through my distrust of you the act of a man penis-ceased, with my lonely physical description of humanity, acting alone.

I was ready in the beginning of this, as you know, but a few days passed and now I despise you, and have shut myself away, and am not ready to accept you.

You were a woman because I am a man; and to please you I pressed my fondness seemingly towards a woman's image. But now I despise you and can freely say, it was all of you.

You are not windmills and I am not Don Quixote; nor am I a windmill for your thrusts, which are not comical but cruel.

When a particular woman took my penis into her body, or all particular women, or he who shook my hand, or—or . . . they all ate at my substance.

This woman used my penis as a calf would use an udder.

If I am powered to child in a woman I will not, I will cast no part of what is human in me again into the world, as I have done since the dawn of man.

And you, (particular) in this my focus, (now), I despise you, because here again I give myself to you.

Will literary criticism serve you?, or will you be that much deeper to the subject I am proposing, namely, that I despise you. It will be easy to say in literary fashion that this, (and you will do it to cover what you know is true), that this is a very negative piece which offers the reader little. (In fact nothing, since of my mentioned feelings towards you!)

I am able, because I have said what I have said in the above, to feel a slight hunger in my hand, so that my penis also hungers vaguely; well—that all my communicative parts stir faintly.

Almost the feeling to erase the above and to begin again with you. But you have hurt me, you have scarred my fondness so many times; so that I will leave the above to hurt you.

I am tempted also to explain something sexual so that you will feel a pang in your loins. I am tempted to tell you what I have done. If I should tell you that women, if they could, would crawl into their own wombs for safe-keeping, that they would shut their eyes and think no more of the world, you might be able to understand the nature of solitude. I am tempted to come even closer in my description than this, and tell you it is quite possible that a man seeks more than entrance into a woman's body, but to be compacted in that body.

(—Divine paradox that a man is so much larger than his penis, and, so to speak, at a right angle to it.)

The pertinent thing is that I acted to shut another gate of my person to you.

The important thing is that I was successful in the act, but that it did not sustain me over the important part of solitude which comes after the "bridge burning," or the gate closing.

As fact, it makes me wonder if any of you (you—particular, reading this) have done this thing. I know you've thought of it. The act is perhaps unimportant, and if that be, of course we are brothers.

But someone past or to come, or even now, has, is, or will do this thing.

Damn you with your rotten literary eye: of course I'm begging the question. Damn you for knowing it. But I can't tell you and you know that too.

Remarkable things have been revealed in our late history through the personal confessions of writers existing in that late history. I assure you, in actual human practice I am a pioneer. (I am not speaking of motive, mind you, but of a practice.)

You will not find this commitment mentioned in Freud or in any of the other investigators of this subject. (If this means anything to you!)

I realize now, that I have dwelled too long without telling you the subject of the above statements. This is unfair to you (although by now you have guessed it, or think you have, but even if you think you have, there is still a doubt; you will never be sure, and it is better that way).
YES, I admit that ultimately it were better that you knew; but also, ultimately that you accepted me, and I know that you won't. So why should I not keep my protection?

It is at last for me to say, that we, or I at least, must learn to balance self and its solitude (and this is the thing to be learned!) with the out-world of you. Like the wearing of clothing. I shall then, dart here and there, always with an away-motion, but touching you slightly; and if you make a motion to hurt, well it's no matter because I was retreating anyway, and the blow is not so hard as you meant it to be. Because I can not live without you—(imagine a man saying this to his wife, for his wife and he are on the verge of divorce); I will suffer the demolition of your scorn and your various impoverishing acts upon my person.

Remember: in the beginning I spoke of her, but meant all of you. (You—particular, reading this now.)

———————————

But now a day has passed, and again I come back to this, hurting badly because of what you have done. I have not even the energy to despise. I know now that I shall live alone and never again suffer you.
—Walking in the autumn, autumn in New England—I shall pause

in the clear air; for then I will have thrown off this hot lethargy of the south, I shall pause in all wonder; for have I not done this before?, will it not be again?

I shall write works that have autumn air between their words.

I shall imagine all sorts of things about you; and write your myth. But never will I again become engaged in your small workings.

I shall dream about Him. And I shall prepare myself for Him; (and He does come!) Do not say, He doesn't, for you do not know; you are too busy working out the small mystery, the mean mystery; and you can not pause in the New England autumn.

There shall be autumn air and old houses through my work. I shall write YOU to the gods, which you are. (But never can be.) Small work made beautiful, and larger than small work, but it is the lore of one. And these things: as cooking a meal, or tending a garden that shall move the world.

The small angle of these works will send out ever widening rays in words.

AND I TELL YOU, YOU SHALL ARGUE WITH MY LOGIC, AND YOU SHALL SEE WITH MY EYES . . . . . you shall drink your coffee in the cups I prefer. . . .

But you will not pause in the autumn as I shall, for it is not given you to know.

I am leaving you, I arise from my small nature and leave you.

I wander not with you, and you shall be lost for my world; till, as it will come, in a flood upon you, and you shall be driven into the streets, by my word.

I say this and in my mind your faces show, pinched by the blight which is upon your souls.

And now you laugh and you laugh, half now I think you weep.

Your faces are red like contagious pimples.

Your faces give forth in a yellow pouring.

What pitiful things are your mouths when they laugh; the lips are loose like the edges of a tent, they flap.

Your laughter is in sound like the fall of man.

Very like a man at the head of a stairway when of a sudden he feels empty, and surely now, for he hears something falling down the stairs; it is he.

Your laughter is like an endless fall down the stairs.

In the autumn I shall restore you. I shall pause and shed with the trees the hot lethargy and clarify in that air of autumn.

You do not believe this, for it is not given you to believe. And that is why I will leave you. And I shall leave no matter where I find you. And I shall find you everyplace, and I shall be in continual rise.

For it is given you to grub out these things that confuse you, things that make you sit with stupid eyes and ugly mouths, things that you can only laugh at.

I will leave you only to save you. Only to write your story. Only to tell Him of you. For though I leave, have I not sprung from you, and do I still not have a fondness for you?

It may be your children and not yourselves who will finger the edges of my works. They shall know (if it is **they**), that here is a treasure that they can not understand; but nevertheless here is a treasure, and so much more a treasure because a human created it.

They shall call themselves human.

They shall marvel at the work of humans, **they** that are given to grub out their own confusion.

Can you see why I shall pause in the New England autumn?
I shall not fear your ambush there, even though I tell you now what I shall do; because, remember, I shall be leaving you all the while, and in my ascent you shall be limited to your confused legs (confused with laughter and what you can never know).

It is not only in the passing of a day that I came to this, it is through betrayal.
And I knew of this, this happening when I traveled through my father into my mother.
I knew it when my mother took me to her breast . . . . . I knew of the betrayal.

And in the autumn

Upward, to be up
My shaggy mistress.
I will not tell.
She, slender stalks, down now comes from;
Whipped with my faster fist.
I've not lost
To be lost again my shaggy mistress.
Weave, oh weave in variousness.
Slenderly, descendingly, mistress, mistress!
From my loins they have hung the celibate rope.
Mistress, my hands, your hands, hands given to the flood,
Whipped with my faster fist –
Faster fist!
Rosy riots of the eyes.
My mistress over in white.
Wearing brown, I bring you to white.
And finally mistress I bring you to white.

the woodland

Silent in the woods where snow is falling
Silent in their hoods where snow is falling
Snow-things
Tree-brown
And lovely snow
White and falling

Under the needled wing snow is falling
Fluffy white oh fluffy flight
In and out the winter night

Came snow and they
And the trees and the rocks
And the houses and the lights
Came snow and they
Through the woods

And light
And through the woods
And red children faces
And winter apples
And light and night.

and snow

Milbury, moth-eaten
Reflected on the cool wind swept –
Where reflected autumns
Of leaves and disproportioned lovers.
Winter) and crags of trees clocked in the wind.
Spring) the birds flew back.
Autumn) the lovers part.
Winter) a whistling despair.
Spring) death among the kisses.

Who Hears? Who Hears?
few years. few years.

Poem

The day is full of blue light –
And sweet piney smell is soon that of flowers.

The air has no height –
And the intertwining vines now cower.

There is a constant pressure wrought by the grass,
Broken only by the long low paths under the evergreen.

The pines are from beneath the earth standing in a huge mass.
And in the dark bowels of the woodland lie the obscene.

Summer Landscape

Quiet place of roof
With grass behind,
Rising from the hairs of bush.
House shapes –
And no voice issues
In complaint –
In the trees one fine day;
Or cool shadowed face, as of a tree,
Shifting of a mass.
The house shape
Makes the distance of like-house shapes.
Opaque winds of trees –
Similar the roof wanders
Among the trees in the distant hair.
And grass green – the trees rise –
And of a sudden the chimneys –
Soon the cloud and the smoke and cloud –
Wire and smoke and wet tangles of a tree,
A street is hidden of a distance –
Green rooves and green trees set in the distance
Where the smoke may hide all –
And the foliage may be red buds.
And the house is seen.
(Who lives in that house?)
She is smiling by a window –
She is looking over a flat bush kneeling by the window
—All night,
She among the rugs and chairs and windows and prints.
Her mother in a window sees a distant man –
A man sees a distant house –
Sees many distant houses and the trees.

And the sun goes –
And she is gone to bed near a shifting tree.
A wasp a fly a white cocoon a moth, living by the window
—All night.
House shapes of a distance
Enthralled in a great shape all treed,
Or may be smoke of unseen chimneys –
In the gutters of a roof may be leaves
And paper or broken nests or shiny twigs.
And if it rains people in the house hear a gentle roar
In the trees –
And on the windows the sputter of rain –
And the flat bush is wet green shining –
And she is smiling on the window
Wishing for thunder.
Summer is a green green house
And now the rain, she smiles.

THE MURDER OF SYLVIA

The accomplice moves west
His head is an absorbent of mist
And Sylvia lies any way
Stopped therein
Where the birds are thin
Sylvia
Pleats of water are quiet

For morning comes in the kitchen
Morning comes where the plants are green
Where the plants may be green
Were they seen
If the kitchen is a cloudy day
Children play
If the kitchen is a window
And the day is pale
For they eat breakfast
With oranges and napkins
And the food may be pale
And the table cloth dull sky
There are fried eggs
With orange yolks and cream-colored whites
And there is milk in a white pitcher
And tiny flowers on the white cloth
And windsor chairs in the kitchen
Where they eat

The light of the day is seen through a cloud
The light of the day is a cloudy crystal
The light of the day is quartz
With minute brightnesses
And dull oranges

And things are shiny
When the light is white
In the living room and the books
when afternoon is come
The afternoon is a cloudy day
And children play
The trees without leaves and comes the rain
And all the trees are in the lane
With grass becoming
And all the trees
In the summer rain
In the early spring when maple-things are growing
Early spring rain

The wall is dark under windows

When screens are rusted
Rusting in the summer
And below
Is a flat bush and the leaves
And a path of stones leads around the house
To the flat bush and the leaves and a path of stones

The sky is come over
The roof
In simple shapes through the flat bush
The sky is white and almost rain
And around the chimney
And nests and antenna-wire and rain and clouds and slate
Of roof and gutters of rain and passive leaves
And still wetness with slow movements of trees
Near the window
Antenna-wire and a nest with rain left in the fall
On the roof when it rains and the clouds

Sylvia is not in her room
She has not come down to breakfast
She is being called
And asked for by the children.

Oh Mother Mother It Is Broken

Oh mother mother it is broken
Trees and day
And leaf taken
And the clatter
And the sky bladder
And mother
And all sky
And all things
Such as things seem

In great catastrophe
That fell on a country road
As hoof beats
As tree shapes
Finally everlasting love
In the sky
In me shapes
And finally the cool gaze
Splintered glass-like
And the liquid world
Like liquid in the eye
Lost shape
And trees and day
Mother and sky
And all things
Converged

And there was love
And boundaries were lost
And the fragilities
Breathed warm again

Oh mother mother it is broken

Rose

Up rose the rosen hill,
Green valley below.
Enter under the twig.
Quick successions of the bird. Enter under the twig.
Rose the malady, white is frozen.
Enter, enter under the flows,
Where under, wet thunder.
The rosen hill, Rose, we upward the rosen hill –
Thunder proceeded, preceding, upward, upward –
Rose after, Rose fore. Rose is my secret door.
Quick skinned flowers by way we go.
White is frozen, hill is rosen,
Valley is below, valley is green below.
I suddenly Rose you love –
I Rose you suddenly love –
Suddenly sudddenly.
Rose the malady, white is frozen –
While snows white flowers –
White blows white flowers.
Upward . . . . Upward Rose to kiss me Rose, upward Rose –
Out of frozen, out of organ, out of white –
Were spring thou flowered white, you kneel upward out of white.
Twine thee to me, thee to me, twined, upward rose up the rose hill

When of sunday, I came by a moth
Describing circles,
Or a child lip-sticking her face
Into enormous color.
Branch of the leaf, or that earth that stays by the root.
And it is this I shun:
The favored look of the outer – and it is **that** I shun –
Here where the forest comes to meet me,
And the earth lies easily on either hand,
Or evening softly with itself,
Over the house. And the garden is at last
The growing dead and dried.
However, the moth describes –
And of sunday, if it be spring, the outer asleep,
Or the child lip-sticking her face
Into enormous color, I shall
Be that new thing older.
I shall be, however the moth describes.
Hear now, the swans fly, necks longer,
Air softer. . . . .

poem

A wingless person walks
On the scopes of land,
Unvisioned as we see,
And rarely so
And so constant of the forest –
Til perhaps the house beyond the sight –
And he submerges in a rock or valley below –
Stumbles on the saplinged hill –
Enters behind a window and is still.

A tremendous bird
Oscillates into birds nicely made;
And with a southern movement the bird is gone –
And with an awkward movement the child is bad.
The earth is gently in the sea with breaking sounds –
The earth is so.
And the remembrance comes at last –
A cockroach is dying in the hall –
Birds approaching –
Through the still twilighted branches of the trees –
Birds approaching –
Birds approaching. . . . .

remembrance

Ralph had a flight machine—O yes, certainly he had!

Martha was his wife; she missed him in the night.

The night was as black as Ralph's dear tie; the night, O lost and vast, strangled where the trees are intertwined; growing in the highlands, rooted in the moss. Trees abhorring the taste of salt that lingers in the lowlands—O lowlands that sip the sea, washed white with foam.

The flight machine in the silken hours, that precede the morning, stayed wait in the sea-cave, O dormant in the centuries till Ralph is come, . . . left Martha in the night in his flight machine, seeking on the ways of sky.

Angel nor devil came beckoning nor threatening. He went with no horror, lest angel soldiers mob him with their brutal wings, without horror of the eviled things that walk as man, to come and cut him down in his retreats, until he come to the fires of his own doing, to watch with clicking teeth and grief sweating in his eyelids and all the secret folds of his docile body, the black regurgitations of all his days burnt grey.

O Ralph has left in his flight machine. In the falling leaves that walked all through the evening period and on into the night—till the first beams of blue fought through the armpits of trees, brought light, where light was needed; and a darker people somewhere retreat from their day into night, breathed heavily with sleep.

Martha, seen blurred through a window glass, cried without tears, with the trees she watched, strangled in her breast.

And Ralph floated, glided as a leaf, though higher than any leaf dare grow. In his flying machine, equipped: with pans and spoons, bedding, glassware and a box of underwear.

The flight machine creaked like trees in the fall, and they, in turn, like the riggings of ships. The flight machine built mainly of alarmclocks and eggcartons sailed gently against the wind.

O Ralph, tell how you come to this oblivion of escape, where no earthly winds shatter the stillness. Why have you brought your flight machine to the earth's vine in a mist specked gold? In the night did you hear voices other than your own, that came whispering intimately in your ear, as you lay close to Martha?

Ralph is a vagabond of the sky, (if only for a night); he listens to voices under the sky, that sound: wings flapping in a tent.

... But the flight machine splintered in the sky, and the underwear dove from their box like men diving from a sinking ship; floated earthward followed by a can of baked-beans.

Poor Ralph descended from the height, through the sky, till he came: where bands of angels, like beads, hung in the sky; chanting replies to the world and its echos.

The flight machine fell through the mist of dawn into the sea, where the crab murmurs: bubbled breath, deep, deep in the black paste of sunless leagues.

The baked-beans splattered on a rock, where the birds giggle, weary in the mist. An now the men, who, headless, footless and without hands, and being truly underwear, sink within the moss as balls of mildewed wool.

Ralph up so high, with angels strung as beads across the sky ... watches his body struggle against the horny-things that seep from sea caves, deeper yet, from hell, looking for the soul. Mutilating the body with horns and barbed tails.

The bat retreating from the day, squeaks, pierced with barbed tail, falls dead in the mist, floats on the sea with its blood coloring the mist, redded steam.

The midday comes without Ralph, and Martha wonders of him, and of the years that bleed across her mind as colored dyes; trees choked in her chest ... where is Ralph?

The midday swallowed by the afternoon, and afternoon on into night, night into day, day into night, and finally, as it will happen, the earth plunged into the sun—and all is burnt, powdered grey ...

Ralph ... Ralph, Ralph!

Ralph's Flight Machine

Hillmann

Hillmann so swiftly, we hardly accept bright offerings offered to Hillmann and we from Hillmann's face.

Child of the afternoon so swiftly ever.

He is friend to man, and mostly Hillmann's friend.

The rejected is walking in the fields of the weeped-world-weeping, unspilling as yet all of himself.

Hillmann, not happy, not anything but Hillmann.

Hillmann's eyes said to us:

I am Hillmann.

DO YOU KNOW US?

I am Hillmann.

BUT, DO YOU KNOW US?

I am Hillmann.

WE KNOW, BUT, DO YOU KNOW US?

You're not Hillmann, I am Hillmann.

THEN YOU DON'T KNOW US?

My name is Hillmann.

Everyday I'm Hillmann.

Hillmann does all kind of everything, and he is.

I'm Hillmann.

And now the slight insistence of the dawn makes known the garden, wherefore the leaves are to the ground.

Pale pinks of dawn; Hillmann climbs over the horizon, as ever a garden wall in sunlight today.

Birds are absent in the morning, and their sound.

Hillmann is being.

Swift call for sleep, now Hillmann is ended, on the leaves ended.
And the birds begun for morning again.
This is the end.
Watch, will Hillman thus extend?
No, he is an end, unextended for he has ended.
Suddenly he is unwith us.
Finished, put him away.
Oh, Hillmann has offered the unoffered.
And not offering the unoffered offering because of the end, we are
lonely, and wish to be offered the unoffered.
. . . And even not accepting this, we still . . .
Or would we now accept?
Hillmann was thus given us, and mostly to himself.

I am unlearnt and slowly to cripple. Cadaver of lips and temple, cheeks for the suction complete. Cleans me, makes me mannered and muddied. Slow cat in my vision, slower that I hardly window soul. Mingle the men-dolls, fingers like the fringe of the shawl. The bliss-night before: . . . stolen by the naughty time.

sleep) The mouse is like a moon, like a moon, like a tone I little heard.

awake) Both of some light like vague fingers, like the smile of Mona Lisa.

sleepy) Oooh, he does not say yes—he wants to go.

sleep) Depleted to the animal and plant . . . when such sights could amuse, . . . make wonder, . . . he concedes all nature natural . . . nourishes on the grants of time and geography. Then something self accounts for the quitting and becoming of something else.

waking) Then told out of wool to regain the graph of calendar.

in the middle of the day) I wonder why a fly forges air. Or why the gadfly will follow to the Nile—and finally why I wonder why I wonder why I wonder?

sleep) In the brown light among the mark of what sing-songs on window . . . astride my organ I shall total all. In the great sill-bed that o'er looks sundom from my nocturn height.

a progress in Disbelief

any one

any one in dull weeks or years of day may eclipse and close.
. . . may snow since first ring of birds—words had marrowed with
spring the winter bones.
now's tower is ice and rue, and tombs such swings, as was what
twinned as twig; as was what made us unalone, as of a field in spring.
the moon, digest the day, bring night, is: any one has lost his day.

any one's tomb is heavy with any one's resistance.
any one will rise once to shout them all down.
once any one will shout, only to shut and cry, as evening whites with
moon, as evening nights; for any one has not the day.

any one will mate early, wifing to dam what wilts.
and courts rummaging his wits for the enticing word.
any one is bored.
any one's wifing bores any one.
any one's wedding night—
any one's wedding at night—
any one in the night of his wedding is any one lost for a day.

NOTES

A branch breathes wind. A branch leads further. A branch and a bud spoon air like a feather; and further leads a leaf that pats a wind. Suppose a man is massed and follow in his ton, like a month upon a day, and the tree is simian?

---

teacher:	How is **birds** spelt?
child:	**Birds spill** on the hands of wind.
teacher:	**Spelt!**—Spell it!
child:	I – T.
teacher:	I, is right; **birds** has no T.
child:	Yet **birds** have a tree.
teacher:	Spell me **birds**.
child:	With a P?
teacher:	With B, like baskets in a tree.
child:	See, **birds do** have a tree.
teacher:	Is B like a branch?
child:	B is where the **birds** of tree . . .
teacher:	Spell me **birds**.
child:	B . . . . . .

Where is my mother? I mean my MOTHER, the large, indescribable one; not my foster flesh one, not my don'ts and restricter one.

Of all suddens, the brackish hour, the black hour, the shower of all clocks among gifts and the keep-sakes and the clips and forget-menots.

Oh, in the tea hour, how a cool cosmic ray casteth . . .

Two girls found at last that their **sensitive** could be expressed by combining their sensitive places.

Birds sing and all daylight is at night.

By combining lip to lip, teat to teat, delta to delta, thigh to thigh, fingertip to fingertip, eyes to eyes . . . . But, eyes to eyes: they see the living soul, the soul living, the coiling brain, the snake in the skull. They part, they part with their pubic hair mixed; their seeings mixed.

Face, east and denting sky: the doting ghost—
Steeds that stride the dandelion, He comes His rival, all lit in His quarrelling gates: ice and sun.

Shadow-me, the lances that pierce far glance.
Clear cloth, leaf path; but moon flees moss-light blind, behind tree wind and mound; and the bell loose, blanks the master fear.
Here wear-sick, man deaf in light, that throbs the flesh.

The light frayed bounce of fan, trend of beast, the metal white falls, walls the shade not beyond the tent of tree.
Nest if quill, and forest quilt.

Salad is a green and glorious death; eat it, turn it earth. Turn your head—Speak; and deliver not the greenery on your breath when you speak so.

. . . Nor rump-steak recall most vivid bull who fought to lead, and

now lies passive to my plate. Nor drapes recall the fields of flax.
Relax, for the wine is not grape nor wine nor sun; nor is anything
..... Speak!

In just a little I am going to grow crow-wing and fly cross county,
flutter through the markets and shatter the concepts of the quiet
evening. That deal of quiet talk inerting what impulse flutters.
Soothing beyond substance. Lady, with her breath squeezed to a
whisper, because the neighbors might hear.
Has like the same insistence of a fly's buzz; though the fly means
nothing to say, so much are they: thievers of oxygen with their
nothing leaks.
But gently, self, for love will meek us all.
But, if once we **night** past all hope that lives of day, we will come
out, neat dressed, on the backporch in the evening, to quietly talk.
In a little, I will kick the neat-polite-thin-middle-aged-lady from her
rocking-throne down the porch steps, where she shall rise in all
manhood, a truckdriver with her expiring politeness, she will curse.

I do not want to write of you like this; I would rather be writing you
a letter of deepest heartfelt sympathy for your ever endurance of my
eyes, and for my body that you bore.
You once said something that I can't remember, I am sure the world
changed because of it.
You once made some gesture that made me love you, somewhere
you did this, I can't remember; but, when you did, I came gladly to
you, and was made warm and human.

In tawny dusk, iodine and day done, eels of limbs co-coil.—She
must decay.

Before an end we sit in the evening, and evening is an end.
And the end is not come.
Evening as an end—Only to rise we again to replace the day.
Heaven darks a million ends only to light, only to resurrect again.
So as internal dross, which is eternity rusting on the organ; the flesh gone before the mind is aware.
As a cat stalks the lone leaf of autumn, becomes lost in winter.
Movie films weep the grief we are yet to weep, so suddenly we are grieving, so suddenly we are older than we were before.
Resurrection was one time: as to take a grief to sleep with us, was one time the new day.
Each time to rise **one** time. **Oh new resurrection!**
With the same grief as day before, we tire of resurrection.

————————

Wilbur grassed after the end; and did we not see a grain flurry?
Indeed, a heavy nature settled over mind; after autumn the snow's seat.
Are you asleep, we ask ourselves, with Wilbur's corpse wretched in the noise.
Wherefore, but that heaven's deep . . . . ?
Do learn the clay?—

Or mend outside of day?

————————

It is each pore misses the corresponding pore of **them** that go.
Somehow, of universe there is a correspondence of star and pore and leaf, and **them** that go.
Somehow, this little toe cramped by that step taken somewhere beyond sight and ear will in my shoe be known.

————————

We fornicated in a tiny light, so many rooms back ago.

I am **obliger** to look into a room where I live, where I can not give my children to Chloe; it is the kitchen, and the ghost mother tends the nourishments, but for the while. At past this, another room gathers for the sight, strewn with lovers, like an ashtray filled with burnt-out cigarettes. And no **love** will restore. Rooms, rooms, beyond all hope.

––––––––––––

If her thigh split and nest a beaked herd, then will I sit, questnot, and serve the scene my eyes; or closet them my lids and dross awhile.

––––––––––––

The economy of single has been dealt with by the spendthrift heart.
(These bloodless terms give distance to the subject)
Thus we come to an inflation of words.
To an inflation of affection in the vacuum of departure, acquiring a stray dog to our withoutness.

––––––––––––

Giant Wednesday comes containing me—While the minutes strain within the hour, whilst the hours spoke the wheel of days—Weeks that can not wive the days—Years that stutter in the mind.
One moment she was knitting lint—One moment—One moment.
But the constipated heart, and dust, and London's doors are made of fog-wood. Continents or keys that jingle in the corridors. . . . .
One moment she was knitting lint and the Wednesday come; and we may come by that to know, eternity begins at Wednesday.

––––––––––––

The sea hangs in itself like a chandelier.
From a hill I thought I thought the sea was a million break of bottles.
But the sea is a liquid wind; the wind so thickened that it crawls

upon the shores.

Arms meet heights his seeks take him, to mingle him down, to single him bound, to lip him all pressed, to quench.
To lose gate!
To open again with cloven wits. Improper gaze of sight's frozen arc. The clean salute of lids walling, fallen from the crag-high greet of cloud, or from the heady heaven sired by the double sweet and swath of sight.
Closes the soon-sad sight in the stricture of an ersatz night.

Sleep, sleep, in the fractures of Paradise.

Man manifest in tree, is wind holder with leaf-shield, greekment here held. Where light through a tree might as through a sandal. He struggles now in new bark health, event-er with summer in a day.
Where if I whisper, whisper couches in the wind's cough and rummage through the trees. Each leaf a door to one certain space, much aside by wind's come.

By stream's side I walk with little winters in my mind.
I walk numbly, minding stream's turn and circle.
Mad, because you can not repeat what you have said, having said it too early, with an innocence bland on infantine lips.

I discovered a wretched little man. He was under my bed. I had thought it a child's hand; the wretched creature was given to child-like extremities.
On being caught thus, he did not excuse himself, but sulked among the drapes.
Odd, I felt no embarrassment. I felt no desire to chase him.

more NOTES

These unravelments mean, I still fuss where I find an easy grave.
Forgive me my articles of poison, play with them as you will, but
beware, these are human things, and filled with pain.
Or else a bird take **fancy**, and fly to our imagined nest. (At nest).
What ever shall we do?

———————————

Down the mouthy rock—Hand fought where the moss sleeps.
The bone of the foot sags in the flesh, in the squinting eye of rock.
He is down coming host of a million fears.
"Goodnight," she hissed.

———————————

Old lady drag my heart up the street with your motherness, your
young-girl-that-I-loveness.
Move up the street and perish out of mind, undo me with forget-
ness.

———————————

Duel man in twilight. Then hope hope hope; the birds on legs now
the birds on legs, and the warm-lament against the ancient chafe of
bills upon, within a hedge, the mucous and the writhe of segment.

———————————

I remember when first I stopped in spring and heard little winters
filling in my mind; then was your name applauded in my lips, as
babbler harlot, I caught all things to heart.
Till land is rust: my autumn come.

———————————

This animal was broken **twice**. This animal's single kingdom shall lack for another. And he shall not distinguish man from woman. But he shall pace in his own skin. And he shall be alone.

———————————

When into her I felt giganticly thawed—Though then, retreat under the heavy cliff of words—Words the cleft and cause the farness.

———————————

Let us create her death too soon for grief.

# of Major-Must

Zebra shadows lean on trail as I off to the one, the major-must of me—the hero sweet, the bleeder in the war rinsed wood.

Now's hour does not tease, though a twin life would not time enough trail's end, me to come.

Great cleanser, ever further than the ever reaching.

How hovering heart in the mid-gates of half belief sustains, is for the see-sawing, almost queasy killed love of problems. Half now I think the feet feel what the head is yet to yield, we are almost dead from the monotony of grass, so we must desert our sated sight. Come us through the crone mountains to a wisdom of their wrinkled cheeks (what ever for?).

I am traveled for the hope that lives beyond stealth, lives in the ruins of the body once young and wrong.

Death ends this trail, I nod, my feet re-lie the new step made, but sooner made they up, repeat, I can not watch as I can not watch the glass of hours.

I must unravel time to come death's sweet, death's major-must of me.

Zebra shadows lean on trail and vibrate on the sight, the door of light only shuts to open, shutting, becomes as like a limping candle's tongue. So hope is as candle's flame, almost out, kindles again against the dark.

Oh my one, I cut from cradle, I cast from modest modes, thee to come. Oh my only, as I looked from autumn through the dying tresses of trees, I think I saw to the end of my single scope, and true for the moan of it all I grieved my absence, for I was not, could not be here, when to you must go, as go **was!**

And thus through the incense of the autumn and the street fights I strove to thee.

Passion I have not, for this I know offends the irony, but love I have, excitement for the gritting of such bones as I bring thee in my flesh. Oh, my one, you turn my heart a clock.

(Put the thorn my way, that I taste trail's end, oh my sweet killer, darling of the space.)

emil

I

I am a child of fifteen, perhaps given to the grand statement.
My calm eyes are brown, but you can tell they are blue by looking at them.
I am not sure who I am, though I try to be myself at all times; except for an advantage, then I emulate somebody else. And even then I am not sure but that the emulation is not really myself.
I am certain that I am attractive to women older than myself.
But it is an annoying thing that I can not remember names; not even my own. People call me by different names I am sure. They do not remember who I am. So be it. I have not done anything of greatness yet.
I am loved by a woman who, though older than I, is but a child. She loves me because she thinks I am a child.
It is when the out-house is in-noised by little birds on the roof; it shall be late at night this time when old men stroll the woods with some filthy image in their minds. And on such nights it is often that the frogs mate. She comes at night.
My father is a farmer. He does not see the beauty of his work, and that is why he is an ugly man.
The old men stroll behind the out-house in the woods, in the broken glass thereof, the poison ivy and amongst the thorn vines that bear neither fruit nor green. They in the midday sun, as I sweat and

everything is moist, they are dry with the dried crisps of voluptuousness in their minds. They know if I am in the out-house. They
are a dirty crew and they smell like shit. And what do they think
when they see me with her?—a child with a man's estate in a woman's eyes.

Though my father does beautiful work he grows the more ugly from
his doing of it.

She is the only memory in the universe, modified only in her love
for me.

She is the only one who remembers myself. She does not call me by
any name; it is always darling or lover. But I would rather the caress.
The thing I can not tolerate is people acting like myself, which they
do continually. I have realized it for a long while that people secretly
admire me. But it makes me angry when people act like forgetting
the fact that it is I they are copying. They even tell me I am copying
them, or putting on airs. Their egos do not permit them the admis-
sion to themselves that it is I they are emulating. So be it. I have not
done anything of lasting greatness. But when I do, let them copy
that and the world will condemn them.

II

I was in the wood shed in the evening—I heard the dry slam of the
door behind me. Hearing the dry tread of the old strollers in the
unwet brush. The sun was setting and cool married shadows raced
over the shed. My father called me for supper. (He has a notion that
I am frail.) I did not answer. I had been thinking: "Here you big
funny world, I am not afraid of you, or any star of you. Big funny
world, my lover's coming. I am not afraid of your soldiers, world. My
lover works for the salvation army, she's a nurse, a famous woman
flier, she's a debutante. Her arms smile around me and I've no care
what you do, world; kill one star or a window light. My lover's on the
walk in the twilight, fumbles with latches and enters. Let the heav-
ens tweak the steeples. Let the world put its tables upsidedown."

The birds sing a paradise till I discover the world crouching by the porch, that awkward animal with loose lips and closed eyes . . . My father called again, "There's a lady here to see you . . . Supper's ready Sonny."

It was not she, it was my mother wearing a new dress . . . . But my memory, my secret heart, she will come later.

I am upset, is my name Sonny? Or have I no name and Sonny is that common endearment the male child answers to?

You understand, she did not come tonight. Oh I explore the torso as I eat supper. My heart and my blood a stranger.

Old men and the moon drift in the woods: For the ships that we are drift away from the other.

A choral from the woods offers me now: "How would you know, soft limbs that you are?"

For it is often that the frogs mate!

"And I," **do you hear it now?** "I was a sensible girl with a respect for my parents and a love for God. I was easy with my movements as the guiltless are. I was a strong girl, and I could cook and could do numbers in my head. GOD DAMN YOU, WILL YOU SIT UP! IT'S ALL OVER YOUR LAP."

Tread softly for the woods are silent.

"Oh, what is that devil that will have its own. . . . ?"

III

Who is myself I have ceased to care about. It is what I will be that matters. And there is time for me to choose a proper name, to choose the proper identity. It is enough that my eyes are brown with their calmness that speaks of blue, if you will notice.

She did not come last night, my lover.

Here it is, twelve noon and I have not decided what I shall be—who I shall be. I can not hold any opinion, for I am not sure if this is myself.

And now the enraged earth rattles, but I hold it back by standing firmly on it—then the train passes and the world hisses.

I am upset by my daily occurrence on the earth; being unsure of everything. Here I am, entering upon my voluptuousness, spied upon by those who have passed through theirs. They have acquired ugly conclusions. My father is a conclusion. I am a sensitive young man. I am a frail child. I am spying upon myself. And I so feel for the nasty crew in the woods. I am an old, old man with a filthy image and a ragged leg. I am a child of fourteen, perhaps given to the grand statement.

My calm eyes are brown, but you can tell they are blue by looking at them.

work in grey

SOFT MOVEMENT IN THE TREES, THE GREY LIGHT ENTERS
ON SLOW ROOMS WHERE FORESTS ARE TO THE WALL—
AND NOW SHADES OF DISTANT GIANTS RISE FROM DIS-
TANT BEDS UPON THE WALL.
THE SLEEPERS HUM, SO QUIET IN THE HALL, SOME PAPER
IN THE HALL MATCH STICKS AND SOME DUST—PARTS OF
THE WEEKS.
THE SLEEPERS' HUM IS STOPPED—THE WIND NOW
WITH STRENGTH THROUGH THE FIELDS APPROACHING
THE ROOMS THROUGH THE LEAVES AND THE BIRDS.
SLOW MOVEMENT AND THE WATER IN THE SINK, AND,
THROUGH THE FOREST. BROWN ANIMALS WITH SLOW
BODIES AND QUICK FEET QUIETLY OVER THE LEAVES
DEVOURING BROWN ANIMALS WITH SPASMODIC BRIGHT
TEETH.
MINUTE MEN DRAGGING LITTLE ANIMALS BY THEIR
PAWS. MEN IN CORDUROY WITH LACED BOOTS AND GUNS
WALKING ON THE LARGE LEAVES COMING OVER THE
GREY ROCK, STUMBLES AND REGAINS THE LEAVES AGAIN:
STRUGGLING IN THE TWIG ERECTIONS TO KEEP THEM
FROM HIS EYES—HE FLAYS HIS ARMS AGAINST THE TWIGS
TEARING HIS MACKINAW FIGHTING TO SEE. HE HAS LOST
HIS GUN AND A BOOT HAS COME UNDONE—AND AT LAST
THE TWIGS TEAR HIS EYES FROM HIS HEAD AND HE SITS
ON THE LEAVES AND HE CAN NOT SEE. HIS CLOTHES ARE
TORN AND HIS BOOT UNTIED. AT DAWN HE HAD STARTED
WARMLY DRESSED WITH WATER-PROOF BOOTS. TWO
GREAT BLISTERS OF BLOOD ARE BROKEN WHERE HIS EYES

ARE MISSING. A SMALL BROWN ANIMAL COMES NEAR TO BE PETTED WITH ITS SHINY NAILS ON THE LEAVES. AND HE PETS IT AS IT LAPS THE BLACK YOLKS OF HIS EYES AMONG THE DUSTY LEAVES. OTHER BROWN ANIMALS PRESSED LOW AND DRIFTING UNDER THE TWIGS COME AND HE PETS THEM AS HIS FINGERS RUB OVER THE MIN-UTE TEETH THEIR SPASMODIC MOVEMENTS HIS HANDS LOSE THEIR DIMENSIONS AS THEY ARE NIBBLED. ONE ANIMAL OF TAUT FLUTES OF FLESH QUICKLY CATCHES THE BRIGHT BUTTONS FROM HIS MACKINAW. HE STARTS TO RISE BUT THE SMALL ANIMALS REST THEIR FORE-PAWS ON HIS SHOULDERS AND PUT THEIR CARESSING TONGUES IN HIS EYE PITS, THEY LICK HIS FACE AND PINCH IT AND LICK AND PINCH TILL SMALL HOLES OF BLOOD ARE, AND THESE ARE LICKED AND ALMOST SUCKED— THEIR TONGUES COME INTO THE UNDERSIDE OF HIS LIPS, HE IS PRESSING HIS THIGHS TOGETHER AND HIS BREAST MUSCLES ARE TRYING TO EMBRACE. HE IS KISS-ING THESE MOUTHS THAT HAVE FOUND HIS OWN.

AGAINST THE SHARP WIND HE LIES TO SLEEP, WITH HIS DRY TONGUE IN THE LEAVES, AND THIGHS PRESSED TIGHTLY, WITH HIS RAGGED HANDS TO HIS CROTCH. WITH ANIMALS ABOUT HIM, THEIR MUZZLES IN THEIR FUR BITING FLEAS, THEIR MINUTE MOUTHS OPENED FOR YAWNING, THEY ARE STRETCHING AND THEY ARE SCRATCHING—SOME WITH BODIES BENT IN CIRCLES ARE ASLEEP.

Silver-Bert

Silver-Bert, boy with two birds and one tower.
Come out of where the world touches.
Silver-Bert in the land of hills will come, no more.
Child of a kingdom done, springs of hair that fall on a forehead, (A forehead dulled white like a wall in a house of seventeen rooms; a wall of a room shut away from the rest; (where we have known the terror alone and never told.) (The winter came and then the summer.)
Silver-Bert in the tower with the birds; (first bird-bits, then the feathers sighted, and the birds come unto him). One for each hand and each hand for either bird.
Bewildered in the window of the tower.
And if in a child's book, the grey tower stands through the black cloud of jam; and oh . . . oh linear Silver-Bert with colors pale.
(Said a child to a child)
"I wonder what he thinks, not looking anywhere and everywhere, he looks, **the too good to be true.**"
This the child said to the child who listened to the child who then spoke first.
(Silver-Bert alive)
  His mother said "cry."
He didn't and he looked.
She hit him where the springs of hair fall jangling, and she said "cry, retreat from your wonder—the wonder that a tea cup has when the daughters of a revolution gather about it, with fingers poised to drink, that, they never drink. Would, that your face a mosaic on a

wall of a secret temple, your face made of children's teeth;—till a quake make your wonder-head the pebbled bed of the river thread. Now I tell you to cry!"

He didn't, and he looked; with birds on his wrists and feathers in his sleeves.

Silver-Bert with round hands and stump-fingers.

(The child peered on the book, fell back in an epileptic fit.)

Silver-Bert with fingers long and thin as insect legs;—the birds found no perch, their feet slipped through and through the linear fingers, like water through the grass. And they perched on his wrists at last.

So the message is written—**come out of where the world touches**.

And Silver-Bert forgotten still wonders though forgotten in the tower.

Birds and hill and sky and fig tree and the Monk in prayer and all things that we ever, when we . . . .

A Man on a Train

A woman on the water front, appeared with packages. She removed her clothing and stood looking at the water.

It is seldom anyone comes here, because the forest is thick.

I came to follow her, she turned from the water from back into the forest. She walked conversing, pleading, and then laughing; at times, almost with surprise she would say, "Really?"

The moon made a bright grey on the forest. She moved with unhurtable grace through the rough branches that seemed to caress her body she as she moved. How beautiful was her body.

I thought she had noticed me, for she nodded in my direction; and I was about to approach when she started to talk to someone, though I saw no one.

Then, in anguish, she cried, "No! why are you going?; it is for you I bare myself, and leave my packages."

"And, it is now," she said, "I feel it within myself."

She clenched the moon out of her eyes as she lay on her back. She wriggled as in pain. I again started to approach, and she sat up giggling. She spread her legs and from between her legs she pulled a toad. I heard her say, "Toby Toad, I am queen of toads." She stood up pulling spiders from her loins, crying, "I am queen of spiders." And all manner of vermin issued thus; wriggled on the ground in the wet of her body, and flew up toward the moon. And the flies settled on her nipples. She was laughing at her profound joke.

"Joy, joy, joy, gently, oh crowd me not." "My insides disgust me." "Take thy mother, here is thy mother." "I am an ocean from whence came . . ." "And I was born of myself, as was my mother . . . . . And I am sick."

And she started to cry. I came to her, and she said, "I've done something awful, what will I tell them; how can I tell them our dreadful sin?"

And then a large animal took her away; and I heard her laughing in the thicket: No, no George, its late, no, George. (more laughter)

Later on old woman came to the house and asked for the night's lodging. She took off her rags, green with moss. Her body: a toad like thing.

She asked me to cut away the toad-stools growing out of her loins; and I cut them away.

And she said that she was my mother and asked me to drink of her breasts; the taste was salty, bloody, like the green juice of plants, like milk, like saliva, the taste of tears. She caressed my hair as a lover. And I reached into the hag-loin: I touched soft earth, there seemed a small valley with a brook. Suddenly I felt the body of a young girl, she wriggled like a snake, she was a snake, and then a girl again. I brought my hand from the other-earth of her womb. She was laughing, the old earth-hag.

And in my sleep I felt her hands in my mouth, her finger in my anus, her rough finger over my eyelids.

The body of all forest surrounded my organ of thrust. And I chanted, mother, mother, mother. There were leaves and twigs in the bed. And in the night a virgin lay in the will of my passion. And I heard the ocean, fisted and footed, kicking the numb shore in the

rhythms of my body; and I turned and was delivered.

And I dreamed of a hag born from a young girl.

And the sea became a sucking baby's lip, and all the world was the foamy digestion of the infant.

And I brightly clothed of leaves, neither slept nor waked, neither woman nor man, devil nor god.

And, at last, I wish for her to bring me home again, sleeped of her arms.

A man seen on a fast-moving train, with his ticket ready and breakfast in his body and . . . . .

words
to
a
garden
wall

"I remember it was Arthur who first had the courage to kill me, thereafter no one tried. They didn't even try to kiss me. No one for a long while has attempted any intrusion upon my person. They have left this garden, nor do I find them in the living room smoking. I find it difficult, for I think I have forgotten how to speak, how to interpret the heart. I am lonely and no flower consoles this; I let the winter confirm it and that gives me some peace."

"Why does no one come? Have I been too anxious to be among my fellows? I had tried to play their game: To be the best in whatever thing I did. And, indeed I was, perhaps too good. For they do not play with me any more. I am out of the running, as it were. Specialized and isolated, and all my talents given to this garden. Surely, you must know I was made for a far better endeavor than the tending of this garden. Surely my flowers are better than any other garden's, but no one comes to see even these. Oh they have worked a better revenge on me, than I ever could've worked on them; they will not look at my good works!"

"They have ruined my courage. Suppose they came, how would I receive them? Would I be able to appear unconcerned, perhaps, slightly annoyed? Or would I run to them, even before they got past the gate to entreat them enter? Would I thus appear so anxious for their company they would have the upper hand? I have quite forgotten how I controlled them of old. Forgotten quite the old defense. And how was I so defensive that they ceased to challenge me? Left me so, as I am, without friend or enemy. And soon I shall be without desire. Without desire to tend, year after year these unconscious flowers, that bear brilliance of sun and pink of clay. However this may be, however foolish my occupation, one day I am less than these. Left alone to die, for they shall not come even then. Shall I be stooping over a flower then? No one comes, you see, and I gradually go into the ground by myself . . . into my garden by myself, less than these. And who is enormous enough to redeem himself ofter this?"

"An old woman grows hair on her face. She is a man at last. (I have no changes to make.) She at last sees the world as mannish, succumbs to this, gives up at last the woman guise. (What changes can I make?) What new thing shall I be, and if so, who shall see? Oh many the nights I have had the wish to follow the rabbits across the fields. You will understand, the dogs attack us there. No, I would not stand and say I am a man; I should face it at last. Let me be a rabbit then, and do not laugh if I look as a man looks."

"How many times have I stood as a tree, or in the attitude of a flower, being neither flower or tree. Where shall I build my kingdom now? A man must build a kingdom, at least once. If a man does not do this he is not ready for death. I am ready for death, but have no kingdom as yet. I have never had a kingdom, that place where the program of desire and fulfillment come manifold as one grows older."

"I can not retire, sick of the world, for I am retired and have a hunger of the world. I am watching myself too closely. I am being destroyed in my own eyes; this is not a good thing for a man to see."

"Tonight the rabbits will come. I shall be a rabbit too. The rabbits and I shall eat this small kingdom of the flowers, that I had made. And the dogs at last . . . Flowers in my intestines and the dogs at last . . . . . Where human hunters come and take us home. . . ."

P. S. "I think to eat us, or for our furs."

in the

How uncomfortable we are. Cold in the damp shifts of the earth. Unlike to anything we see. Uncertain in all acts, no matter how slight. Muffled by the great discomfort into an off-vision, till we be dream-like. Dreamers in the afternoon in casual terms. Say, shall I listen by the finger-shadows of the trees near the windows of the parlor?

And who was there? The neighbor's little girl, her aunt, Miss Secund, and others I will not remember for I can not. Let me try . . . large plants that dwindled to their roots into pots, the leafage is immense, the talk in the afternoon as of the underwater, light of the sun that twinkles the dust till one hardly dare breathe lest the dust score the breath tube.

afternoon

The little girl wandered over the parlor touching things. I was annoyed with her movements; Annoyed because the child attracted parts of myself in nervous twitches, almost to begin her activity, which I had no want to do. I was there at last. I looked at myself as I had looked at the group talking their nonsense. But I am I; **unsmall, unmask, unhint**, but fully wet and blood-flowed. And I watched myself, **it** was hungry, I mean **I** was hungry. And that hunger is questionable. It does not curl up and go to sleep with some tidbit dissolving in its tract. And so I thought of food, but it was not this. I thought of women, undressed them, put them in different land-scapes; Added children to these landscapes, filled the children with lust or innocence as that mood would have; But I was unfavored, if favor is to be had. Thus the hunger stayed to upset my later activities unquenched.

I was fiddling with some red flower, and suddenly I had ruined it. I hoped they would not notice, for they "oooooh" and they "what have you done to the pretty flower?" crucifying one with their whines.

The little girl had a gadget she had picked up in the parlor, and was trying vainly to make it perform; It had a crank and a handle . . . It may have been a can-opener.

I said, give it here. She continued struggling with it. I put my hands on it and started to turn the crank. She was pulling on it and I said again, give it here . . . here . . . this is how it goes.

There was blood on my hands, perhaps I had pricked my finger on the stem of the flower.

I was determined to find out how the gadget worked so the little girl would stop fussing with it.

The blood was on her hands now and all over the gadget. I was having difficulty holding it. I was confused because the people were looking. I could not let the gadget go and have the people see the little girl out-smart me finding out about the gadget. I was ashamed of my blood and waited for their "ooooohs." I felt ugly, as though involved in a crime. Miss Secund said, "Let the man have it." Did she mean for the child to hit me? If she meant for the child to let it go, I did not want this, that I should seem the bully. It would have been too easy a victory. Finally I let go and the child fell. The others did not notice this. The child was embarrassed and stuck her tongue out at me. I don't know why, but I returned the gesture. I rubbed the blood off my hands on the rug. I was annoyed because the child's hands still had my blood on them. The child was soiled with my blood. What would the others say?

She wiped it on her white dress.

**end
ceremonial**

Russell Edson

Russell Edson (December 12, 1928 – April 29, 2014), often referred to as "the godfather of the prose poem in America," was a poet, novelist, and illustrator. He was the son of cartoonist-screenwriter Gus Edson, best known for his work on two popular, long running comic strips, *The Gumps* and *Dondi*.

Edson studied art early in life and attended the Art Students League of New York as a teenager. His first collection of poetry and short fiction, *Ceremonies in Bachelor Space*, was published in 1951 by Black Mountain College. In the early 1960s, he self-published several chapbooks of prose poems under the imprint Thing Press, the best of which were later collected into *The Very Thing That Happens: Fables and Drawings*, published by New Directions in 1964. Numerous other collections followed, as well as a book of plays, *The Falling Sickness*, also published by New Directions (1975). Throughout his career, his work appeared in countless anthologies and literary magazines. He was awarded a Guggenheim Fellowship (1974), The Whiting Award (1989), and three National Endowment for the Arts Creative Writing Fellowships (1976, 1981, 1992).

Acknowledgments

Profound thanks are extended to the following for their generous financial support which helped to defray some of production costs of this new edition:

Danielle Alexander, Adrian Astur Alvarez, Álvaro Pina Arrabal,
Gregory K Baer, Thomas Young Barmore Jr, Nick Barry,
Matthew Beckham, Joseph Benincase, Cameron Bennett,
Dudgrick Bevins, Brian R. Boisvert, Anthony Brown,
Hannah Carroll, Tobias Carroll, Scott Chiddister, Adam Cloutier,
C. Colla, Menachem Cohen, Christopher Ty Cooper,
Joshua Lee Cooper, Sheri Costa, Nancy Vieira Couto,
Parker & Malcolm Curtis, Albie D., Robert Dallas, Thad DeVassie,
Joel Deusterman, Dave "Wahoo" Eckard, Curtis B. Edmundson,
Royce Engemann, Rodney David Falberg, John Feins, GMarkC,
Elizabeth O. Hackler, Frank 'Faft' Hagen, Ashley Hamm,
Kyle P. Havenhill, Erik Hemming, Aric Herzog, Kaarina Hollo,
Jonathan Hope, G. Alexander Hyphen, William Jarvis,
Jakob Inooraq Johannesen, Erik T Johnson, Kristiana Josifi,
Haya .K., Handsome Ryan Kennedy, Larry Kerschner,
M.D. Kuehn, C. S. Labairon, David Leiman, Giles Leonard,
Gardner Linn, LordHog, T.B. Lucas, Josh Mahler,

Michael S. Manley, Theodore Marks, Thomas McCarthy,
Jim McElroy, Sergio Mendez-Torres,
Dr. Melvin "Steve" Mesophagus, Spencer F Montgomery,
Josh Montoya, Serpent Moon, Geoffrey Moses, Gregory Moses,
Séamus Murphy, Richard Ohnemus, Michael O'Shaughnessy,
Danny Paige, Brandon Anthony Pinter, Pedro Ponce,
Stephen Press, Patrick M Regner, Kara Roncin & James Wheeler,
Glenn Russell, George Salis, Christopher Sartisohn,
Kristen Scanlan, Connor Shirley, Fawn Siemsen-Fuchs,
Michael Skazick, Joslyn Sklar, Neil Smalheiser, Adam V.,
Cato Vandrare, Christopher Wheeling, Isaiah Whisner,
Karl Wieser, T.R. Wolfe, The Zemenides Family,
and Anonymous